HELLO KITTY®

Hello Seasons!

ABRADALE

New York

Today is the first day of a new year at school. Hello Kitty tries on her new outfit. It fits! Mama packs her a lunch and she's ready to go.

When she gets to class, Hello Kitty picks
a desk at the front of the room near her
friends. The teacher asks the class to write
about their favorite season. Hello Kitty
doesn't know which one to pick.

In the fall, Hello Kitty likes to go apple picking at a nearby farm. She climbs up the trees to get the apples on the highest branches.

Pumpkin picking is lots of fun, too. Hello Kitty
chooses a big one so that she can carve a
friendly jack-o'-lantern face.

Fall is also harvest time. Hello Kitty helps
Grandma pick tomatoes, peas, and eggplant
from the garden.

On weekends, Hello Kitty and her friends like to jump in leaf piles. They take some pretty red and purple leaves home to make a center-piece for the table.

In the winter, snow days are the best.
Hello Kitty and Mimmy play in the snow,
go sledding, and make snowmen!

Mama makes hot chocolate for them when they come inside. Yum!

When it's too cold to play outside, Hello Kitty likes to write letters to her friends. She sends one to Dear Daniel, one to Jodie, one to Thomas, and one to Fifi. She sends the special heart-shaped card to Grandma.

Winter vacation is coming up soon. Hello Kitty
looks forward to ice skating with Fifi.

In the spring, Hello Kitty can go outside without a jacket. She sees the tulips starting to sprout. They are always the first ones to pop up.

Spring is great for trips to the park. Hello Kitty and Mimmy like to have a picnic and watch the clouds turn into different shapes. What shape do you see? Hello Kitty sees an elephant. Mimmy sees a kangaroo.

There are so many fun things to do in the summer. Hello Kitty likes to meet her friends in the park for a game of baseball. She brings everyone a sunflower from her garden.

On the way home, everyone always stops for
an ice cream cone!

Hello Kitty could spend the whole summer at the beach. She likes to build sand castles and then snorkle in the water.

She also likes to play catch with her friends!

There are so many fun things to do in every season. Hello Kitty is still having trouble picking her favorite one. She likes them all. She decides she likes whatever season she is in, best.

She takes out her pencil and writes about fall.
Even though the leaves will soon be falling off
the trees, it always feels like a new beginning.

ISBN 978-1-4197-0652-3

Text, illustrations, and original art copyright © SANRIO CO., LTD.

© 1976, 2013 SANRIO CO., LTD. Used Under License. www.sanrio.com

Published in 2013 by Abradale, an imprint of Abrams. All rights reserved.
No portion of this book may be reproduced, stored in a retrieval system,
or transmitted in any form or by any means, mechanical, electronic, photocopying,
recording, or otherwise, without written permission from the publisher.

Printed and bound in China
10 9 8 7 6 5 4 3 2

THE ART OF BOOKS SINCE 1949
115 West 18th Street
New York, NY 10011
www.abramsbooks.com